HOW TO TELL A
MYTH

Robert Walker

🍄 Crabtree Publishing Company

www.crabtreebooks.com

Text STYLES

Author: Robert Walker

Coordinating editor: Reagan Miller

Publishing plan research and development:
Sean Charlebois, Reagan Miller
Crabtree Publishing Company

Editorial director: Kathy Middleton

Print coordinator: Katherine Berti

Production coordinator: Margaret Salter

Prepress technician: Margaret Salter

Logo design: Samantha Crabtree

Product development: Victory Productions, Inc.

    Content Editor: Janet Stone

    Photo research: Tracy Vancelette

Front cover: Featured characters from various myths include: Anubis, the jackal-headed Egyptian god of mummification and the afterlife; One of "The Hours", or Greek goddesses of the seasons, who were attendants to Venus; a dragon from the Nine Dragons Scroll, painted in 13th century China; and the goat-drawn chariot of Thor, the Norse god of thunder.

Title page: A small world coming into creation from the void of space.

Photographs:

Circa Art: 14 (forest)

Corbis: Stefano Bianchetti 19

Digital Stock Professional: title page (night sky)

Wikimedia Commons: cover (Sandro Botticelli, Uffizi Gallery: Birth of Venus; Chen Rong: The Nine Dragons handscroll; Tanngrisnir and Tanngnjostr by Frølich; Nyo: Thor's hammer)

Shutterstock: All other images

Illustrations:

Barbara Bedell: 13 (tortoise)

Bonna Rouse: 13 (hibernating bears), 18 (arrows), 29 (porcupine)

Margaret Amy Salter: 14 (owl and ocean run sockeye)

Ole Skedsmo: 23 (Greek man)

Cataloguing in Publication data available at Library and Archives Canada.

Cataloging-in-Publication Data available at Library of Congress.

Crabtree Publishing Company
www.crabtreebooks.com   1-800-387-7650

Printed in Canada/082011/MA20110714

Published in Canada
Crabtree Publishing
616 Welland Ave.
St. Catharines, Ontario
L2M 5V6

Published in the United States
Crabtree Publishing
PMB 59051
350 Fifth Avenue, 59th Floor
New York, New York 10118

Published in the United Kingdom
Crabtree Publishing
Maritime House
Basin Road North, Hove
BN41 1WR

Published in Australia
Crabtree Publishing
3 Charles Street
Coburg North
VIC 3058

Contents

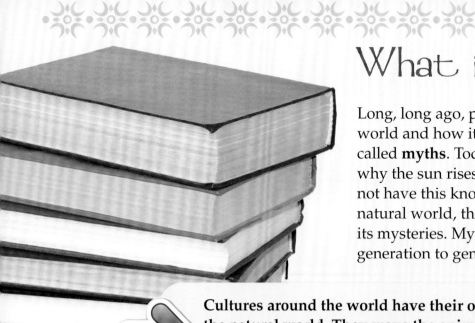

What is a Myth?

Long, long ago, people told stories about the world and how it came to be. These stories are called **myths**. Today, we have science to tell us why the sun rises and sets. Early people did not have this knowledge. To understand the natural world, they told stories that explained its mysteries. Myths were passed down from generation to generation.

Cultures around the world have their own myths to explain the natural world. They wove the animals and features of their natural world into stories of magical creatures and events. **Their beliefs and values are reflected in their myths.**

Where do myths come from?

Most myths have **heroes** who perform great feats and deeds. Many myths also have powerful gods and goddesses. Gods and goddesses have power over human beings. They could help humans and other characters, or punish them for their behavior.

Why do people tell myths?

Myths teach us life lessons. Heroes in myths show us how to behave. We learn to treat people and the natural world with respect. We learn the lessons about kindness, sharing, and courage.

In this book, you will learn about the characteristics of myths. You will read myths from different cultures and even write a myth of your own!

Old Man Coyote Makes the World

The Crow are a Native American people that lived originally in the western United States. A Plains nation, they hunted bison across the huge stretches of prairie lands. Native people lived very closely with nature. They treated the world and everything in it with respect. Their relationship with the environment shaped how their myths were told.

The Crow people believed that the world was created by a being called Old Man Coyote. Old Man Coyote was a spirit with supernatural powers. In the beginning Earth was covered in water. There was no dry land to be found. Old Man Coyote saw this world of water and it made him sad.

"I can't find anyone to talk to," he said, looking across the endless oceans. "There is only water, and I am completely alone."

So Old Man Coyote set out to see if there was some place dry to sit and someone to keep him company.

"Hello there!" Old Coyote called happily to two ducks. "I am very glad to have found you."

Old Man Coyote spoke with the ducks for a while. He asked them, "Do you think there is anything else on Earth other than water?"

The ducks, who were excellent divers, said they believed there was something deep under the water. So Old Man Coyote told them to dive as deep as they could and see what they could find.

So the ducks dove under the water. They were gone a very long time. Old Man Coyote began to worry that they may have drowned. Then suddenly they returned to the surface. They were very excited.

"We have found something!" the ducks told Old Man Coyote excitedly. "It was hard and different than water." They presented old Man Coyote with what they had found.

It was the root of a plant, Old Man Coyote saw. He was very pleased, so he asked the ducks to dive down again to see if they could find anything else. The ducks did so, and soon returned with a small lump of soil.

"Wonderful!" cried Old Man Coyote. "I will use this dirt to make land." So he took a deep breath and blew on the small bit of dirt. It grew and grew and soon began to spread over the water. He then took the root the ducks had found and planted it in the new ground. Many things began to grow. There was grass and trees and all sorts of plants.

Old Man Coyote was pleased. But he noticed that all of the land was flat. There needed to be more.

"Well, why don't you carve out different shapes in the ground?" suggested the ducks. "You could make hills and mountains and canyons as well as flat ground."

Old Man Coyote agreed. So he set about shaping the world. He made tall mountains, long flat plains, and islands, too. He even carved out rivers and lakes for his duck friends.

Old Man Coyote and the ducks looked at his work. They all agreed it was wonderful. But there was still something missing, thought Old Man Coyote.

"My brothers, now the world is more than just water. But it is still very quiet," said Old Man Coyote. "I think we need other creatures to keep us company in our new home."

So Old man Coyote grabbed a ball of dirt and began to shape people out of it. He made men and women, and spread them out across the ground.

The ducks asked if Old Man Coyote would make them some friends as well, so he did. Old Man Coyote made more ducks. He also made all sorts of other creatures: buffalo, deer, bears, and elk.

Old Many Coyote then filled the world he had made with music and sounds. He gave the people drums and made birds to sing sweet melodies. Soon the world was full of dancing and laughter.

There was also fighting and stealing too, but Old Man Coyote knew this was a part of life as well. The two ducks thanked Old Man Coyote for making the world, and swam off with their new friends.

Characters in a Native Myth

 Most Native American myths have characters **that are from the natural world. Animals such as crows and bears are able to talk and have supernatural powers. Some of these special creatures were believed to be spirits, or gods, by Native people.**

Old Man Coyote was one of these spirits. He was a very popular character in many Native myths. He was also portrayed in different ways. In some stories he was the hero. In others he was a trickster, or a **villain**. The tricksters and villains in a myth make trouble for the other characters in a story.

Characters, good and evil, can play a large part in a myth or smaller parts. In this story Old Man Coyote is the lead character. The main character gets the most attention in a story. He is the hero faced with a problem. The world is nothing but water and he is lonely. He is also a spirit, with great powers that he can use to solve the problem.

 The two ducks Old Man Coyote meets are called minor characters. The minor characters in a myth play an important role in the story. Minor characters often move a story forward through their actions or words. For example, it is the helpful ducks who assist Old Man Coyote in his quest to create the world and other living things.

The audience learns about characters by their descriptions in the story; how they look, what they wear, and what kind of creature they are. We can learn a lot about characters from their **traits**, or how they act. The good guys will always do the right thing. They will try to help others, be honest, and act bravely. The bad guys will try to make trouble for the main characters with violence, lying, and cheating.

Old Many Coyote then filled the world he had made with music and sounds. He gave the people drums and made birds to sing sweet melodies. Soon the world was full of dancing and laughter.

Old Man Coyote agreed. So he set about shaping the world. He made tall mountains, long flat plains, and islands, too. He even carved out rivers and lakes for his duck friends.

While the story "Old Man Coyote Makes the World" does not have any villains, we can still learn a lot about the other characters.

- What do we know about Old Man Coyote?

- What do we know about the two ducks?

Old Man Coyote	The Two Ducks
• a coyote	• ducks
• powerful spirit	• helpful animals
• enjoys living things	• powerful swimmers

 Describe a Character

Stories tell us a lot about a character—but they still leave a lot to our imagination. We know that Old Man Coyote is a coyote. A coyote is a wild dog that looks like a wolf. But Old Man Coyote is a magical animal. How would you imagine he looks? Does he walk on his hind legs? Does he wear a magic cloak? Write down some additional descriptions of what you think he would look like.

Dialogue and Dialect: What and How It Is Said

 The dialogue **in a myth is what characters say to one another. Spoken words in a story are indicated with quotation marks.**

Dialogue helps us learn more about a character. It makes a myth more interesting. We can learn a lot about a character by what they say and how they say it. We can see if they are happy, sad, or angry. Listen again to what Old Man Coyote says at the beginning of the story:

 "I can't find anyone to talk to," he said, looking across the endless oceans. "There is only water, and I am completely alone."

"We have found something!" the ducks told Old Man Coyote excitedly.

From his words we can gather that Old Man Coyote is a character who enjoys the company of other beings. We can also tell that he is a person who likes variety. He finds a world made only of water sad and boring.

The first example shows us how not all dialogue in a story is spoken to other characters. Sometimes a character will talk to themselves, letting the reader know what he or she is thinking.

With the exclamation point and the word "excitedly," we can see in the second example that the two ducks are happy. They are pleased with what they have discovered, and are anxious to tell Old Man Coyote the good news.

 Dialect is the kind of talking that is specific to a people in a time and place. It is the way characters speak. Some characters speak very formally, using proper grammar. Others speak more casually. Different people speak in different ways. It is how they say things that we can learn where and when they are from.

 "My brothers, now the world is more than just water. But it is still very quiet," said Old Man Coyote.

In modern day, most people do not address friends with something like "my brothers." This way of speaking is usually reserved for characters in stories that took place a long time ago.

Setting: Time and Place

Setting plays a big part in how the story is told. Even though this is make-believe, if the combination of setting and story is too ridiculous, you end up with a silly story. If you were to add lasers and robots to a myth set in the time of knights and castles, chances are you would lose the reader.

Most myths take locations we would recognize, such as on Earth or in the sky, then change the details so it is no longer reality. The setting may be in an entirely made up world altogether. The story of "Old Man Coyote Makes the World" takes place on Earth. But it is a very different planet than the one we know.

The setting **of a myth is the time and place where the story is set. It includes elements like climate and landscape, as well as the era, or period of history. Setting is like the stage in a theater, with all of its different props and backdrops.**

In the beginning, Earth was covered in water. There was no dry land anywhere.

We know today that there was never a time when Earth was nothing but water. There has always been some kind of land here. But myths are rarely based on facts. It is possible that the Native people saw what looked liked endless ocean, and mistakenly believed that at one time the world was actually covered in water. This is a creation myth. How could you tell the story if everything was already created?

Write it Down: Setting Details

Think of a setting for a myth. Where and when will it take place? Make a list of the details for the setting of your story. Be sure to include details about the landscape, including mountains, rivers, and any man-made structures.

The Plot of a Myth

Every myth has a beginning, a middle, and an end. The events in each part make up the plot. First, the characters are introduced. We learn things about the characters, like how they look and what kind of person they are.

The main characters must face a problem or challenge. This problem sets the events of the myth in motion. Often, a villain tries to interfere with the main character's progress, usually by setting up obstacles. The events of the myth are all of the action that takes place in the story. They show how the problem is solved.

The plots of most myths are full of action and excitement. The hero might battle scary monsters and travel to strange and interesting places. Because early stories were spoken instead of written down, they had to keep the audiences' attention. The excitement slowly builds up as the story goes along. The moment of greatest excitement is called the **climax**. Myths end shortly after the climax.

This part of the story is called the **resolution**. We find out what happens once the problem has been solved, as well as the fate of the characters of the story.

As a creation myth, "Old Man Coyote Makes the World" does not have a lot of excitement. Its purpose is to explain more than entertain. But it does follow the same format as other myths.

Story Map
A story map can help you outline your myth.

 climax

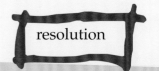 resolution

 events

 characters setting problem

Beginning: Old Man Coyote is lonely and tired of a world with only water.

Event: Old man Coyote comes across the two ducks and asks them for help. They find a root and some dirt under water.

Event: Old Man Coyote uses the dirt to make the ground, and plants the root to create the trees and other plants.

Climax: He then uses more dirt to make humans and other creatures. He also creates music and dancing.

Resolution: With his work done, Old Man Coyote lets the world continue on its natural course.

Plan a Myth

Think of an event that happens in the natural world. For example, bears sleep all winter. How did these things come to be? Write some events that occur in nature that you could explain in a myth. Plan a plot that begins with a problem. The events lead to the resolution. In a Native American myth, a bear raced a turtle and lost. The bear sleeps all winter to forget his humiliation!

Theme: What the Myth Means

While the plot is the chain of events in the story, the **theme** is the main point of the tale. Using characters and events, the story teaches the reader a lesson or an idea. Even though myths come from different peoples from different times and places, a lot of myths share the same themes.

A common theme of early peoples' myths were explanations of the world around them. Using stories with magic and make-believe, people tried to explain the history of the natural world. Early people did not have the understanding of the world that we have today. This is why many of their myths are so colorful and creative. They had to rely on their imaginations to come up with answers.

Myths teach lessons that everyone can use. These include honesty, kindness, charity, and courage. These are lessons that show us how to live and how to treat each other.

The ducks then asked if Old Man Coyote would make them some friends as well. And so he did. Old Man Coyote made more ducks. He also made all sorts of other creatures: buffalo, deer, bears, and elk.

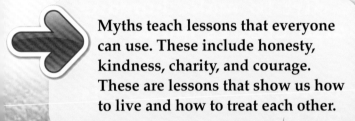

Finding the Theme

The main theme of "Old Man Coyote Makes the World" is creation. But there is another theme as well. In the last paragraph of the story, it says: "There was also fighting and stealing too, but Old Man Coyote knew this was a part of life as well." What is the lesson that this part of the myth is trying to say? Write down your answer and share it with a partner.

Creative Response to the Myth

Put it to Music

Take the story of "Old Man Coyote Makes the World" and make it into a song. Set your words to the tune of one of your favorite songs.

Act it Out!

Get together with some of your friends and perform a short play about "Old Man Coyote Makes the World." Give everyone a part, and even add props if you can. Include lots of action so the audience will pay attention.

Another Point of View

Write a letter from the point of view of one of the creatures Old Man Coyote created. Who would you choose? An owl? A shark? Think about what your letter would say. Would you thank Old Man Coyote for his work? Maybe offer some criticism?

The First Superhero

If it is excitement you are looking for, then look no further than ancient Greece!

Angry gods, giant monsters, brave heroes—the myths of ancient Greece are thrilling tales of danger and adventure. Living almost 3,000 years ago, the ancient Greeks were terrific storytellers. But these were more than just stories to them. Their myths were a big part of their beliefs.

The ancient Greeks believed in many gods. In fact, they believed there was a god that controlled every part of their world. The Greeks believed the gods controlled everything from the ocean to farming.

They also believed their gods had a direct influence on humans, which is the basis for many of their stories.

Most myths from ancient Greece were used to teach valuable life lessons, such as playing fair and sharing. Perhaps the most famous stories from ancient Greece have to do with a hero named Hercules.

Hercules was one of the first superheroes. In Greece, he was known as Heracles, but he is better known around the world by his Roman name Hercules. He was half god, half mortal and stronger than any man.

The Twelve Labors of Hercules

Long ago in ancient Greece there was a man named Hercules. He was the bravest and strongest man alive. His father, Zeus, was a very powerful god. His mother, Alcmene, was a mortal.

When he grew up, Hercules wanted to find a way to use his powers to help other people. He went to talk with an oracle for advice. Oracles were very wise people.

"You must go see King Eurystheus," said the oracle. "Serve him, and take on any task he gives you." "For how long?" asked Hercules. "You must go and serve King Eurystheus for twelve years," answered the oracle.

So Hercules left to see the king. But what he didn't know was that Hera, the wife of Zeus, was jealous of Hercules. Hera had told the oracle to send Hercules to serve King Eurystheus. She knew the king was also jealous of Hercules, and would treat him badly.

When Hercules met with King Eurystheus, the king gave him twelve tasks. He told Hercules that when he had completed them, he was free to go.

"First, I want you to kill the lion of Nemea," ordered Eurystheus. The lion was a giant beast whose skin could not be pierced by any weapon.

Hercules set out for Nemea. He found the angry lion in its cave. Hercules knew his sword was useless against the lion, so instead he used his strength to defeat the beast, beating it down with his fists.

Next the king sent Hercules to slay a hydra, a nine-headed monster whose heads grew back if you cut them off. The blood of the hydra was also poisonous, but Hercules had a plan. He cut each head off with his sword, then used a torch to burn the necks so the heads couldn't grow back. He then dipped his arrows in the hydra's poisonous blood.

"This should make my arrows even more deadly," said Hercules. "This could be of use to me someday."

King Eurystheus was surprised when Hercules returned. He had hoped the hydra would have killed him. *I must find more dangerous tasks for him*, thought the king.

So the jealous Eurystheus sent mighty Hercules on more dangerous quests. These included capturing the wild Erymantian Boar, claiming the red oxen of Geryon, the three-headed giant, bringing back the wild horses of King Diomedes, and stealing the magic belt of Hippolyte, queen of the Amazons. For most of his quests, Hercules did his best not to hurt any of the creatures or people—unless they tried to hurt him first.

Hercules was also sent to slay the man-eating Stymphalian birds, who had sharp metal feathers. Hercules was able to bring down the deadly birds using his poison-tipped arrows.

"It's a good thing I thought to dip my arrows in the hydra's poisoned blood," said Hercules, pulling back on his bow.

King Eurystheus was furious! For his next task, Hercules was ordered to clean the king's oxen stables. With only one day to do it, Hercules used his strength to bend two rivers so the water would flow through the stables. The rushing waters cleaned the dirty stables in no time.

King Eurystheus had only one job left. *I have to find a way for him to fail*, thought the evil king. He thought long and hard. Then a terrible idea came to him.

"For your final quest, I want you to bring me Cerberus," said Eurystheus. "And you must do it without weapons or armor."

"Cerberus? But he is the three-headed dog who guards the gates to the Underworld," said Hercules. "He is one of the fiercest creatures in all creation."

"Does the mighty Hercules not believe he can accomplish this task?" asked Eurystheus, mockingly.

Hercules saw that the king was a bad man. But he was still one task away from earning his freedom from the king's service. Hercules set off to face Cerberus.

Hercules met Cerberus at the gates of the Underworld. The snapping jaws of the three-headed dog were fast—but Hercules was faster. He dodged the monster's attack and wrapped his arms around it. Hercules then wrestled Cerberus to the ground. The beast yelped in surrender.

"Do not fear, hound," said Hercules. "I won't hurt you. And after a quick visit to Eurystheus, I will return you to your post."

Victorious, Hercules returned to Eurystheus with Cerberus slung over his shoulder. The sight of the three-headed monster scared the king. He begged Hercules to take it away.

"I will," laughed Hercules. "But first you must release me from your service. I have completed your twelve tasks and so have earned my freedom."

"Yes, yes, of course!" said Eurystheus, cowering in fear from the horrible dog. "You are free to go."

Hercules returned Cerberus to the gates of the Underworld. He was now free. He would go on to have many more adventures.

* Eurystheus [yoo-RIS-thee-us] * Cerberus [SIR-burr-us]

Heroes and Villains

Hercules is a great example of a hero. The heroes in myths are bigger, stronger, and smarter than ordinary people. They try to help people and stop the evil-doers. In this myth, the villians are Hera, King Eurystheus, and the monsters Hercules must face.

Hercules uses his superpowers like strength and speed to defeat them. He also displays a lot of the traits, such as courage, that make a character a hero. Traits are behavior that a character displays in a story.

What heroic traits does Hercules show in the story?

Kindness

Bravery

Strength

HERO

Sympathy

Resourcefulness

All of these words can be used to describe the actions of Hercules in the story. Now read the sections of the story below, and match them up with the traits that they show.

When he grew up, Hercules wanted to find a way to use his powers to help other people.

Kindness

He then dipped his arrows in the hydra's poison blood. "This should make my arrows even more deadly," said Hercules.

Bravery

He found the angry lion in its cave. Hercules knew his sword was useless against the lion, so instead he used his strength to defeat the beast.

Sympathy

Hercules was also sent to slay the man-eating birds with sharp metal feathers.

Resourcefulness

"Do not fear, hound," said Hercules. "I won't hurt you. And after a quick visit to the king, I will return you to your post."

Strength

 Create Your Own Hero

Develop a hero for a myth. What special traits will your hero have? Heroes do not have to be strong, like Hercules. What special powers could you give your hero? Create a word web of character traits. Let one trait lead you to another. Then circle the traits that you think will best define your hero.

Dialogue: Mind Reading

You have seen some of the different uses of dialogue. It can move the story forward, explain what is happening, and tell the reader about the character. But not all dialogue is spoken. Some characters think it without saying it out loud. Internal dialogue is usually marked with italics.

By "hearing" what a character is thinking, we get a very honest look into their personality. This is very helpful when it comes to tricksters and villains. More often than not they are lying to the other characters in a story.

King Eurystheus was surprised when Hercules returned. He had hoped the hydra would have killed him. *I must find more dangerous tasks for him,* **thought the king.**

King Eurystheus had only one job left. *I have to find a way for him to fail,* **thought the evil king. He thought long and hard. Then a terrible idea came to him.**

Being able to read the thoughts of a villain lets the reader know who the scoundrels are. It also can increase the tension of a story. When the reader knows the truth before the hero, it leaves them anxiously waiting for the hero to find out as well. This is an excellent way to keep the audience interested.

Finding Your Voice

Imagine that you are one of the monsters Hercules faced in this myth. Do some additional research into the character to find out more about it. Then write a letter to Hercules as if you were that monster. What would you say?

In Ancient Greece

The time and setting plays a very important role in "The Twelve Labors of Hercules." The where and the when is ancient Greece. The myth of Hercules was written in the time and place when people believed in monsters like the hydra, and gods and goddesses like Zeus and Hera. It was also a time when people used antique weapons such as swords, shields, and bow and arrows.

Here are some parts of the story that depend on the setting of ancient Greece:

- Oracles were very wise people. Hercules asked the oracle what he should do.

- His father, Zeus, was a very powerful god.

- The theft of the magic belt of Hippolyte, queen of the Amazons.

Compare Settings: Then and Now

You have read about the time and place of ancient Greece in a myth. Now imagine a myth set in modern day. What would be some of the differences in setting? What would be some of the similarities? Complete the chart below to compare a myth from ancient Greece to how a myth from today might look. Consider things like locations, buildings, and people.

Ancient Greece	Modern Day
hydra	*mad scientist*
temple	
Amazon Queen	
oracle	
arrows	
three-headed dog	
the Underworld	

A Great Adventure

We have already learned that the plot is the basic outline of a story. The events that happen follow the outline, from beginning to end. Early on we learn about the different main characters. We are introduced to the heroes and the villains.

We also learn what the problem or problems are that the heroes must solve. As the plot develops, different events show us how the main characters deal with different problems. This moves the story along. It also shows us what kind of person a character is by how he or she deals with a problem. For example, if the character tries to find a peaceful solution instead of resorting to violence, we learn that he or she is smart.

All of the events in a story lead to the climax. This is the high point of the story: the hero defeats the dragon, the detective solves the crime. Climaxes usually take place near or at the very end of a story.

What follows the climax is the resolution. This is when all the problems have been solved; when all the action is over. This is when many stories reveal the lesson or theme of the tale. Also, the readers usually learn what happens to all the characters afterward. One of the most popular resolutions is, "they all lived happily ever after."

Whatever the story's plot, there needs to be a spine that the events follow. Sometimes it helps to write out a story map of the events when planning a story.

Mapping Your Myth

What sort of events will take place in your story? How will it begin? How will it end? Use a story map like the one on page 12 when charting your story. Make sure to write down everything that will happen in your myth.

Life Lessons

The two myths you have read in this book have different themes. One is a tale that tries to explain the natural world. The other tries to teach the reader important life lessons about courage, kindness, and sympathy.

Hercules is a man faced with an incredibly difficult task. He also has people (a king and a goddess) working against him, trying to keep him from accomplishing his task. He must rely on his strength and cunning in order to succeed.

Throughout the story of Hercules, we see the hero display many positive traits. Gifted with tremendous powers, Hercules wants to find a way to use them to help others. Even though he must fight horrible monsters, he kills them only when he has to.

Hercules also displays courage when he goes off to complete these dangerous tasks. During the course of them, he uses quick thinking to succeed.

These are all excellent behavior traits that would help serve people in their everyday lives.

 An Important Message

What will the theme of your myth be? Choose a theme or lesson you feel is important and valuable for people to learn. For example, you could focus on courage or kindness. Try to come up with several possibilities and list them.

Creative Response to the Myth

A Myth Review

Imagine that you live in ancient Greece. You have heard a storyteller tell "The Twelve Labors of Hercules." Write a review of the myth. Talk about the parts you enjoyed and the parts that you did not.

Superheroes: Then and Now

You have read how Hercules was the original superhero. Can you think of any other modern superheroes that are like Hercules? Explain how this superhero is like Hercules. Tell how he or she is different.

A Greek Rap

Make a rap song out of the Hercules myth. Not all of the twelve labors were listed in the story. Do some research and find out what all twelve of them were. Then do a rap about them in the order they happened—and do not forget to rhyme!

Writing a Myth

Prewriting

You have read two myths and explored their different parts. Now it is time to write a myth of your own! What kind of myth will you write? Will there be lots of action? What kind of theme will you use? Will it take place in the past or the present? The choice is yours. This chapter will help guide you through the writing process. Be creative, and most importantly, have fun!

1 Choose a Topic

First, decide what kind of story you will be telling. Some things to consider:

- **Are you writing a creation myth, explaining a part of the natural world?**
- **Will your myth teach the reader an important life lesson?**
- **Who will be your audience? Are you writing for adults or young readers?**

2 Explore Your Character

Will your hero be a god or goddess, or a mortal? What heroic traits will your hero have? What will your main characters be like? Decide how they will look, speak, and behave.

3 Setting

Where and when will your myth take place? What values and beliefs do the people of this period hold?

4 Map It Out

Be careful to plan out your myth before you start writing it. Look back at the two story maps from earlier in the book. Make sure you have a beginning, a series of events, a climax, and a resolution. Sketch out your plan on a piece of paper. Pretend your story is a chain, and each part is a link in that chain.

Write a First Draft

With all of your information in order, write up a first draft of your myth. Do not worry about mistakes. Focus on getting your story down on paper. Be sure to have your character, theme, and plot notes handy as you write. These will help keep you on track.

Heroic Myth Checklist

- Do I have a hero with strong traits?
- Do I show the hero's traits through actions?
- Does my myth contain dialogue?

Creation Myth Checklist

- What part of the universe will your main character be creating?
- What is the motivation for your character?
- Does the ending tell how something came to be?

Deanna has chosen to write a creation story. She first introduces the hero of her tale, Porcupine. She has then outlined the problem that Porcupine will have to solve. Read the beginning of her first draft.

How the Porcupine Got His Quills

Porcupine was a small animal with smooth fur. He lived in the fores, and one day he was out looking for food. Sometimes he stole food from the bears. He was small and fast and sneaky. He could even climb trees and steal honey.

One day he climbed a tree to get some honey. He got honey all over him. A bear growled. "That's my honey!" roared the bear. The procupine was scared. He slipped from the tree. He tore his claws on the way down and then landed into a big pile of sharp pine needles. They stuck to his fur. Oh, no! cried the porcupine. He tried to climb back up the tree but he could not. He tried to shake the pine needles off but he could no.

"Go away, Porcupine," said the bear. "You stole food. Now you must be stuck all over with needles. And you can't climb trees anymore."

And that is how the Porcupine got his quills.

6 Revise Your Myth

Read through your myth. Try to add more dialogue and descriptions wherever possible. Make sure that the problem in your story is clear to the reader. Make your changes on a fresh sheet of paper.

Deanna made some changes to the beginning of her myth. She corrected errors in punctuation and spelling. She also added details.

How the Porcupine Got His Quills

Porcupine liked being small and sleek. He could steal food from other animals and run away quickly. With his sharp claws he could climb trees to eat honey. He lived in the forest, and one day he was out looking for food. Sometimes he stole food from the bears. He was small and fast and sneaky. He could even climb trees and steal honey that the bears liked to eat.

But one day when he climbed a tree to get some honey, he got honey all over him. A bear growled. "That is my honey!" roared the bear. The porcupine was so scared that he spilled sticky honey all over him. He slipped from the tree. He tore his claws on the way down and then he landed into a big pile of sharp pine needles. They stuck to his fur.

"Oh no!" cried the porcupine. He tried to climb back up the tree but he could not. He tried to shake the pine needles off but he could not.

"Go away, Porcupine," said the bear. "You stole food. Now you must be stuck all over with needles. And you can't climb trees anymore."

And that is how the Porcupine got his quills.

7 Proofread Your Draft

Take another look at your story. How is your spelling? Are there any sentences that seem to run on for too long? Does the dialogue tell the reader about the characters? It is a good idea to have a dictionary and a thesaurus handy for this part.

- **Do you have run-on sentences or sentence fragments?**
- **Did you capitalize proper nouns?**
- **Did you use dialogue to tell the reader about the characters?**

Deanna proofread her creation myth. She fixed her spelling and grammar mistakes. She also trimmed down the too-long sentences.

How the Porcupine Got His Quills

Porcupine liked being small and sleek. He could steal food from other animals and run away quickly. With his sharp claws he could climb trees to eat honey that the bears liked to eat, too.

But one day when he climbed a tree to get some honey, he heard a bear growl. "That is my honey!" roared the bear. The porcupine was so scared that he spilled sticky honey all over him. He slipped from the tree. He tore his claws on the way down and landed in a big pile of sharp pine needles. They stuck to his sticky fur.

"Oh, no!" cried the porcupine. He tried to shake the pine needles off but he could not. "Please, Bear, do not eat me," he cried.

The bear looked at all those sharp needles. They would hurt me, he thought. He did not want to eat that porcupine! So he said, "Go away, Porcupine. You stole food. Now you must be stuck all over with needles. And you can't climb trees anymore."

That is how the Porcupine got his quills.

Make a Final Copy

You have made your corrections. Now it is time to write your final draft. Use a separate sheet of paper. Share your folktale with a partner. Feel free to add some illustrations to go along with your story.

Glossary

character	A person in a story
climax	The peak of a story
dialect	The particular way people speak
dialogue	Spoken words in a story
event	Something that happens
hero	A brave and noble person
mortal	Human and able to die
myth	A traditional story, usually involving the supernatural
plot	the chain of events in a story
resolution	The closing of a story
setting	Where and when a story takes place
story map	A diagram that shows the basic parts of the plot
theme	The main idea or lesson in a story
traits	A person's behavior
villain	An evil person

Index

Further Resources

Books:

Classic Starts: Greek Myths by Arthur Pober Ed.D (Afterword), Diane Namm (Editor). Sterling Publishing Company (2011)

Golden Tales: Myths, Legends, and Folktales from Latin America by Lulu Delacre. Scholastic (2001)

Illustrated Stories From The Greek Myths by various authors. Usborne Publishing Company (2011)

World Myths and Folktales by Carolyn Logan (editor). Holt McDougal (2002)

Websites:

This site explores the heroes, gods, and monsters of Greek mythology.
www.mythweb.com/

This site presents popular myths in script form so readers can act out the myths as they read.
www.kidsinco.com/myth/

This site includes myths from around the world as well as a writing workshop with a real myth writer!
teacher.scholastic.com/writewit/mff/index.htm